95
Pounds
of
HOPE

Anna Gavalda

translation by Gill Rosner

VIKING

VIKING
Published by Penguin Group
Penguin Young Readers Group, 345 Hudson Street,
New York, New York 10014, U.S.A.
Penguin Books Ltd, 80 Strand, London WC2R 0RL, England
Penguin Books Australia Ltd, 250 Camberwell Road,
Camberwell, Victoria 3124, Australia
Penguin Books Canada Ltd, 10 Alcorn Avenue,
Toronto, Ontario, Canada M4V 3B2
Penguin Books (N.Z.) Ltd, 182-190 Wairau Road,
Auckland 10, New Zealand

First published in France by Bayard Éditions Jeunesse, 2002,
under the title *35 kilos d'espoir*.
Published in the United States of America by Viking,
a division of Penguin Young Readers Group, 2003.

1 3 5 7 9 10 8 6 4 2

Copyright © Bayard Éditions Jeunesse, 2002
Translation by Gill Rosner, copyright © Penguin Group (USA) Inc., 2003
All rights reserved

LIBRARY OF CONGRESS CATALOGING-IN-PUBLICATION DATA
Gavalda, Anna, date-
[35 kilos d'espoir. English]
Ninety-five pounds of hope / by Anna Gavalda; translated by Gill Rosner
p. cm.
Summary: From his first day, school had been torture for Gregory and it
got progressively worse, until he was expelled in eighth grade, but
through all his difficulties, Gregory could count on support from his
grandfather, until his grandfather became ill and needed support from Gregory.
ISBN 0-670-03672-2 (hardcover)
[1. Grandfathers—Fiction. 2. Learning disabilities—Fiction.
3. Self-realization—Fiction. 4. School—Fiction.] I. Title.
PZ7.G2347Ni 2003 [Fic]—dc21 2003010103

Printed in U.S.A.
Set in Esprit
Book design by Teresa Kietlinski

*To my Grandpa
and to Marie Tondelier*

• • •

1

I hate school. I hate it more than anything in the world. And even worse . . .

It's ruining my life. Until I was three, I could say that my life was happy. I don't really remember that much, but I think things were okay. I would spend my time playing, watching my *Little Brown Bear* video over and over, drawing pictures, and making up hundreds of adventures starring

Big Doggy, my stuffed dog, whom I adored. My mom told me that I used to spend hours in my room giggling and chatting away to myself. So I guess I must have been happy.

At that time in my life, I loved everyone and I thought that everyone loved me. Then, when I was three years and five months old, wham! School.

Apparently, in the morning, I was quite happy to go. My parents must have gone on about it all through the summer:

"You lucky boy, you're going to school. . . ."

"Look at this lovely new schoolbag! It's for your lovely new school!"

And blah blah blah. . . . Apparently, I didn't even cry. (I am the curious type. I think it's because I wanted to see what kind of toys they had, especially Legos.) When I came home at lunchtime, I was enchanted. When I had eaten, I went into my room to tell Big Doggy all about my marvelous morning.

Well, if only I had known, I would have

paid more attention to those last minutes of happiness, because right after that, my life got off track.

"Time to go back," said Mom.

"Where to?"

"To school of course!"

"No."

"No what?"

"I'm not going."

"Oh? And why not?"

"Because I already went. I saw what it's like, and I've done it. I have hundreds of things to do in my room. I told Big Doggy that I was going to build him a special machine for finding all the bones he's buried under my bed, so I don't have time to go to school."

My mother knelt down beside me, and I shook my head. She spoke more firmly, and I started to cry. She picked me up, and I started to scream. Then she slapped me.

It was the first slap of my life.

There you are.

That was school for you.

The beginning of the nightmare.

I've heard my parents tell this story a million times. They've told their friends, my kindergarten teachers, my middle school teachers, psychologists, speech therapists, and career advisors. And each time I hear it, I remember that I never did build that bone detector for Big Doggy.

•

Now I'm thirteen, and I'm in sixth grade. Yes, I know there's something wrong. I'll tell you right away—don't bother to count on your fingers. I stayed back twice: third and sixth grades.

School always causes scenes at home. You can imagine. . . . My mother cries and my father yells, or the other way around, my mother yells and my father says nothing. It really drives me crazy to see them like that, but what can I do? What can I say in a situation like that? Nothing. I say nothing, because if I open my mouth, it's even worse. There's only one thing the two of them ever say to me, and they repeat it like a couple of parrots:

"Work!"

"Work! Work! Work!"

"Work!"

Okay, I understand. I'm not a complete moron after all. I would like to work; the problem is I can't. For me, it's like they teach everything in Chinese. It goes in one ear and out the other. They have taken me to thousands of doctors: eye doctors, ear doctors, even brain doctors. Their conclusion after these wasted hours of consultation: I have a concentration problem. Attention Deficit Disorder—ADD. You have to be kidding! I know exactly what's wrong, and it has nothing to do with concentration. I have no problem. Not a single one. It's just that school doesn't interest me. It doesn't interest me at all, and that's all there is to it.

•

There was just one year when I was happy at school. It was in kindergarten, with a teacher named Marie. I will never forget her.

When I think about it now, I tell myself that Marie must have become a kindergarten teacher to be able to spend her time doing what she liked best in life: building and creating things. I loved her from the beginning. From the first morning of the first day. She wore clothes that she had made herself, sweaters that she had knitted herself, and her jewelry was all made by her. Not a day went by that we didn't take something home: a pâpier-maché hedgehog, a cat with a bottle of milk, a mouse in a walnut shell, mobiles, drawings, paintings, collages. . . . Marie didn't need to wait till Mother's Day for us to get our hands dirty. She would say that a successful day was a day when you made something. When I think about it, I wonder if my happiness with Marie was also the reason for the unhappiness that followed. It was then that I realized a simple truth: nothing interested me much except my own hands and what I could make with them.

I also know what I owe Marie. Thanks to her, I managed to get through kindergarten reasonably well. She had understood what made me tick. She knew that having to write my name brought me to the verge of tears, that I took nothing in, and that for me, reciting a nursery rhyme was pure torture. At the end of the year, on the last day, I went to say good-bye to her. I had a lump in my throat and could hardly talk. I handed her a present. It was a great little pencil box with one drawer for paper clips, another for thumbtacks, a place for the eraser and everything. It had taken me hours to get it right and to decorate it. I saw that she liked it, and she felt as moved as I did.

She said, "I have a gift for you too, Gregory."

It was a fat book.

She added, "Next year, you'll be in Mrs. Daret's class. You're going to have to try very hard. You know why?"

I shook my head.

"To be able to read everything that's in here."

When I got home, I asked my mom to read me the title. She took the huge volume on her knees and said, "*1000 Activities for Little Hands*. My goodness, I can see the mess already!"

I hated Mrs. Daret. I hated the sound of her voice, the way she acted, and the fact that she always had favorites. But I did learn to read, because I wanted to make the hippopotamus out of an egg carton on page 124.

On my final school report from kindergarten, Marie had written, "This boy has a head like a sieve, magic fingers, and a heart of gold. We should be able to make something of him."

It was the first and last time in my life that I received a compliment from a member of the educational system.

2

Anyway, I know plenty of people who don't like school. You, for example. If I ask, "Do you like school?" you'll shake your head and tell me no, of course not. Only major goody-goodies would say yes, or the ones who are so smart that it's like a game for them to test out their intellectual skills every morning. Otherwise . . . who really likes it? Nobody. And who really hates it?

Not that many either. Except the ones like me, the ones they call losers, the ones who always get sick to their stomach.

•

I open my eyes at least an hour before the alarm clock goes off, and for that hour I feel the knot swelling up in my stomach. When I get down from my bunk bed, I feel so sick that it's like being on a boat on the high seas. Breakfast is torture. In fact, I feel like I can't swallow a mouthful, but since my mother is always standing over me, I take a couple of dry crackers. In the bus, my stomachache turns into a hard stone. If I meet friends and we start talking about Zelda or some other game I feel a little better, and the stone gets lighter; but if I'm alone, it suffocates me. The worst moment of all is when I arrive at the school door. It's the smell of school that makes me sick. The years go by and the places change, but that smell stays the same. That mixture of chalk and old sneakers

11

grabs my throat and sends my heart into the pit of my stomach.

The stone starts melting away around four o'clock, and by the time I get back to my room at home, it has completely disappeared. It comes back when my parents get home and start asking me about my day and rifling through my schoolbag to check out my homework book. But with them it's not so bad, because I'm used to their little scenes.

Well, not exactly. I'm not telling the truth. I can't get used to it. Fight after fight, and I still can't stand it. It's really ghastly. Since my parents don't love each other that much anymore, they have to have a fight every evening; and because they don't know how to start off, they use me and my bad grades as an excuse. They blame everything on that. Then my mother blames my father for never having taken the time to do things with me, and my father replies that it's all her fault for spoiling me rotten.

I'm fed up, so fed up. . . .

I'm fed up more than you could ever imagine.

When it's like that, I block my ears from the inside and I concentrate on what I'm building: a Lego spaceship for Anakin Skywalker, or a K'Nex gadget for squeezing toothpaste tubes, or a giant pyramid of old boxes and cartons.

Then comes the torture of homework. If my mother helps me, she always ends up crying. If it's my father, I always end up crying.

I'm telling you all this, but I wouldn't want you to think that I have terrible parents, or that they take it out on me. It's not that at all. My parents are great. Well sort of. . . . I mean, they're just normal. It's school that ruins everything. Actually, last year I only wrote down half the homework in my notebook. I did it to avoid all those evenings of misery. That was the only reason, but I didn't dare say so to the school principal the day I found myself in her office in tears. Stupid really.

Anyway, it was just as well I kept quiet. What could that fat old turkey have understood? Nothing obviously, because the following month she expelled me.

She expelled me because of P.E.

I have to say that I hate P.E. almost as much as class. Not quite as much, but nearly. If you could see me, you'd understand why judo mats and I don't go together. I'm not very tall, not very coordinated, and not very strong. I'd go even further: I'm not very tall, not very coordinated, and I have the muscles of a teddy bear.

Sometimes I stand in front of the mirror with my hands on my hips, puffing out my chest. It's quite a shock. I look like a worm doing bodybuilding or like Popeye before he eats his spinach.

But still, I can't let absolutely everything in life get me down. Something's got to give; otherwise I'd go completely crazy. And that something last year was P.E. Even writing these words makes me smile ear to ear. Mrs. Berluron and her P.E. class always sent me into hysterical fits of laughter.

This is how it began:

"Dubosc, Gregory," she said eyeing her notebook.

"Yes."

I knew that once again I would mess up the gym routine and look ridiculous. I wondered when it would all end.

I stepped forward. The others were already beginning to giggle. But for once, they weren't laughing at my lousy performance. They were laughing at how I looked. I had forgotten my gym things, and since it was the third time that term, I had borrowed Benjamin's brother's clothes to avoid getting detention. (I have had more detentions in one year than you will ever have in your whole life!) What I hadn't known was that Benjamin's brother was a clone of the Jolly Green Giant, and was six feet tall.

So, there I was strutting along in a size XXL tracksuit with size ten sneakers. Needless to say, I was an instant hit.

"What on earth is this getup?" yelled Berluron.

I put on my innocent look and said, "I can't understand it Mrs. Berluron. Last week it fit perfectly. I don't see . . ."

She looked like she would explode.

"Do a double somersault, feet together. Right now!"

I did one catastrophic somersault and lost one sneaker. I heard the others laughing, so to entertain them, I did another one, and managed to send the other shoe flying toward the ceiling.

When I got up, my underpants were showing, because my pants had slipped down. Mrs. Berluron was bright red, and my classmates were cracking up. The sound of that laughter made me feel good. For once I wasn't being made fun of. This was laughter like you hear at the circus, and from that moment on, I decided to be the gym class clown. Mrs. Berluron's court jester. Making people laugh gives you a warm feeling inside, and it's like a drug: the more people laugh, the more you want to make them.

Mrs. Berluron gave me so many detentions that there was no more room in her grade book. In the end, I got expelled because of all that, but I don't regret it. Thanks to her, I did feel a tiny bit happy at school, just a tiny bit useful.

I have to say that I caused total chaos. Before, no one wanted me on their team, because I was so pathetic, but afterward, they fought over me, because my pranks threw the opposing team off. I remember one day when they put me in as goalie. What a scene. . . . As the ball came toward me, I shimmied up the net of the goal like a panic-stricken monkey, yelling in terror. And when I had to put the ball back in the game, I always managed to throw it the wrong way and score a goal for the other team.

Once I even lunged forward to get the ball. Of course, I didn't get near enough to touch it, but when I got up, I was munching a tuft of grass, mooing like a cow. That day Karine Lelièvre peed in her pants, and I got a two-hour detention. But it was worth it!

I was expelled because of the horse. Actually, it's ironic, because for once, I wasn't kidding around. We had to jump onto this huge foam-rubber thing, grabbing hold of the handles. When my turn came, I missed, and really hurt my . . . well you know what I mean. My willy was crushed to a pulp. Of course everyone thought I'd done it on purpose, and I was faking the "Owwww" to make them laugh. Berluron dragged me straight to the principal's office. I was doubled up in pain, but I didn't cry.

I didn't want to give them that pleasure.

My parents didn't believe me either, and when they heard I'd been kicked out for real, I got what was coming to me. For once they were screaming in harmony, and they certainly put their hearts into it.

When they finally let me go back into my room, I shut the door and sat on the floor. I told myself: "Either you climb into bed and cry—and you'd be right to cry because your life is worth nothing, and neither are you, so you might as well cut your losses and die right now—or you get up and make something." That evening, I constructed a giant monster out of a bunch of scraps that I had found on a building site. I called it "Hairy Bery," after my favorite gym teacher.

It wasn't the best joke in the world, I grant you, but it did me good, and at least it kept my pillow dry.

3

The only one who was any comfort to me in those days was my grandfather. It's not surprising, considering that my grandpa Leon had always been the one who made me feel better, ever since I was old enough to go into his workshop.

Grandpa Leon's workshop was my life. It was my hideout, my Ali Baba's cave. When my grandmother started getting on our nerves, Grandpa would wink at me and whisper, "Gregory, how would you like a little journey into Leonland?"

And we would tiptoe off while my grandmother grumbled, "Go on then! Fill the kid's head with nonsense."

He would shrug his shoulders, answering, "Please, Charlotte, please, Gregory and I are leaving because we need a bit of peace to think."

"To think about what, if it's not asking too much?"

"I think about my past, and Gregory thinks about his future."

My grandmother would turn her back, adding that she would rather go deaf than listen to such rubbish. And Grandpa Leon always replied, "But sweetheart, you already are deaf."

•

Grandpa Leon is as good with his hands as I am, but he is smart, too. When he was at school, he was a regular champion. He was always at the top of the class, and he told me that he had never studied on Sundays. ("Why? Because I didn't feel like it, that's why!") He was the best in math, French, Latin, English, history, everything! When he was seventeen he was accepted into the hardest college in France. After that, he designed huge projects: bridges, highways, tunnels, dams, etc. Whenever I asked him exactly what he did, he would relight his cigarette and think out loud.

"I don't know. I have never known the precise definition of my job. Let's say that they ask me to look over plans and tell them what I think. Is the thing in question about to fall apart, yes or no?"

"Is that all?"

"Is that all, is that all? It's important, you know! If you say no, and the dam falls apart just the same, you really feel like an idiot, believe me!"

22

My grandfather's workshop is the place where I am happiest in the world. It's not much: just a hut in the backyard made of planks and corrugated iron. It's too cold in winter and too hot in summer. I try to go there as often as possible. To make things, to borrow tools or bits of wood, and to see Grandpa Leon at work. (At the moment he's making something for a restaurant.) I go to ask his advice or for no reason at all. Just because I like being in a place that feels right.

I told you about the smell of school that made me feel like throwing up; well, in the workshop it's the opposite. When I'm in that overcrowded shack, I breathe in deeply and smell happiness. It's the smell of oil, grease, the electric radiator, the soldering iron, putty, tobacco, and all the rest. It's delicious. I promised myself that one day I would manage to distill it, and invent a perfume called "Eau de Workshop." Then I could smell it whenever life got me down.

•

When Grandpa Leon found out that I was staying back in third grade, he took me on his lap and told me the story of the tortoise and the hare. I remember exactly how I snuggled up to him, and how soft his voice was.

"You see, nobody bet a penny on that pathetic tortoise, she was far too slow. But in the end she won the race. Now, do you know how she did it? She did it because she was a brave little tortoise who never gave up. And you too, Toto, you are brave and determined. I know that, because I've seen you at work. I've seen you spend hours and hours in the cold, sandpapering some scrap of wood or painting one of your models. I think you're just like the tortoise."

"But they never ask us to sandpaper at school!" I cried in reply. "They only ask us to do things that are impossible!"

When Grandpa Leon found out about sixth grade, it was a different story.

I arrived at their house as usual, and he didn't reply when I said hello. We ate in silence, and after coffee, he made no sign of moving.

"Grandpa Leon?"

"What?"

"Shall we go to the workshop?"

"No."

"Why not?"

"Because your mother told me the bad news."

" . . . "

"I can't understand it. You hate school, yet you do everything to stay there as long as possible. . . . "

" . . . "

"But you're not as stupid as they say! . . . Or are you?" His voice was harsh.

"Yes, I am."

"Oh, that attitude really gets on my nerves! Obviously, it's much easier to say that you're no good, and do nothing! Of course! It's just fate! It's so easy to think it's some kind of destiny! So now what? What do you intend to do now? Are you going to repeat seventh, then eighth, and with a bit of luck, you'll get to college by the time you're thirty?"

I fiddled with the corner of a cushion, not daring to look up and meet his eyes.

"No, really, I don't understand you. In any case, don't count on good old Leon anymore. I like people who take their life into their own hands! I can't stand lazy people who wallow in self-pity and get themselves expelled because they have no discipline! It doesn't make sense! Expelled and staying back. Good for you! What a picture! Congratulations! When I think that I have always been on your side . . . Always! I told your parents to have confidence in you. I made excuses for you. I encouraged you! I'll tell you this, my friend: it's easier to be unhappy than happy in this life, and I don't

like people who take the easy way out. I
don't like complainers! Be happy for Pete's
sake! Just do what you have to do to be
happy!"

Then he started coughing. My grandmother came running, and I went outside.

I went into the workshop. I was freezing.
I sat down on an old oil drum and wondered
how I could take my life into my own hands.

If I could spend all my time building
things, I'd be happy, but there was a slight
problem: I had no idea where to start, no
plans, no model, no materials, nothing. All I
had was a huge weight inside which kept the
tears from flowing. I carved something on
my grandfather's bench with my penknife
and went home without saying good-bye.

4

At home, the crisis went on for longer and was even more agonizing than usual. It was the end of June, and no junior high school was prepared to take me in September. My parents were racking their brains and tearing their hair out. As for me, I shrank a little further into myself with each day that passed. I told myself that if I became small enough not to be noticed, I might even disappear completely, and all my problems would disappear with me.

I had been expelled on June 11. At first, I hung around the house all day. In the morning, I would watch infomercials, or QVC (they always have unbelievable things for sale), and in the afternoon I reread old comic books or worked on a 5,000-piece jigsaw puzzle that Aunt Fanny had given me.

But I soon got bored. I had to find something to do with my hands. So I started looking around the house to see if there was anything I could improve. I had often heard my mother grumbling about the ironing, saying that her dream was to be able to do it sitting down. I decided to attack the problem.

I unscrewed the base of the ironing board, the part that stopped Mom from being able to put her legs under it. I calculated the height, and I attached the board to four wooden legs like a normal desk. Then I took the wheels off an old cart that I had found on the sidewalk the week before, and put them on a chair that we didn't use anymore. I even rigged an iron rest for the new iron she had bought. The whole job took me about two days.

Next I dealt with the broken lawn-mower motor. I took it apart, cleaned it, and put all the parts back. It worked perfectly. My dad hadn't believed me when I said so, but I knew it wasn't worth taking it back to the garden center. All it had needed was a good cleaning.

That evening at dinner the atmosphere was less stormy. To thank me, Mom made my favorite dish, grilled cheese sandwiches, and Dad didn't turn the TV on.

He was the first to speak.

"You know, son, the sad thing about you is that you *do* have talent. So what can we do to help you? You don't like school, I know. But school is mandatory until you're sixteen. Did you know that?"

I nodded.

"It's a vicious circle: the less you work, the more you hate school; the more you hate school, the less you work. . . .What are you going to do?"

"I'll wait till I'm sixteen, and then I'll get a job."

"You must be dreaming! Who on earth would hire you?"

"No one, I guess, but I'll invent things. I'll make things. I don't need much money to live on."

"That's what *you* think! Of course you don't have to be rich, but you'll still need more than you realize. You'll need to buy tools, a workshop, a truck, and all sorts of other things. Never mind. For the moment, let's not worry about the money. That's not what bothers me. Let's talk about school. Gregory, don't make that face, look at me please. You won't get anywhere without a minimum of education. Imagine you invent some fantastic thing. You'll have to take out a patent, won't you? So you'll have to be able to write it up properly. And anyway, you can't just come up with an idea for an invention and bingo! you're finished. You'll need to draw up plans, done to scale with accurate measurements, if you want to be taken seriously, otherwise someone else will steal your idea in two seconds."

"You think so?"

"I don't think so, I'm sure."

This bothered me; somehow in all my confusion, I felt that he was right.

"But Dad, you know, I've got one . . . an invention which could make me and my children rich, even you maybe."

"What is it?" asked my mother with a smile.

"Promise to keep it top secret?"

"Yes," they said together.

"Swear."

"I swear."

"Me, too."

"No, Mom, say, "I swear.""

"I swear."

"Well, it's this. . . . Shoes specially made for people who go hiking in the mountains. These shoes would have a little movable heel. You'd put it in normal position while you're going uphill, you'd take it off on the level ground, and you'd put it under your toes to go downhill. That way your feet would always be well balanced, and hill climbing wouldn't be so hard."

My parents nodded in approval.

"That idea of his isn't so dumb," said Mom.

"You should get in touch with a sporting goods store."

I was pleased that they seemed to be taking an interest in me. But the spell was broken when my father added, "But if you want to sell this marvelous invention of yours, you have to be good at math, at computer science and economics. You see, we're back where we started, it's what I was saying before. . . ."

•

Until the end of June, I kept myself busy doing useful odd jobs. I helped our new neighbors clean up their garden. I pulled up so many weeds that my fingers were swollen and green. My hands looked like they belonged to the Incredible Hulk.

Our neighbors were Mr. and Mrs. Martineau. They had a son named Charles who was only a year older than me. But we didn't get along. He was always playing videogames or watching dumb TV reruns, and every time he talked to me, he asked me what class I would be in next year. It got to be more than a little irritating.

Mom continued to call around trying to find a private school that would agree to accept me in September. Every morning we received tons of brochures in the mail.

Photos on glossy paper boasted the merits of this or that school.

They were all pathetic and completely untrue. I leafed through them, shaking my head, wondering how they had managed to get photos of the students smiling. Either it was bribery, or the kids were being told that their teacher had just fallen over a cliff. There was only one school I liked the look of, but it was too far away, somewhere near Valence. In the photos, the students weren't sitting behind desks smiling idiotically. They were in a greenhouse potting plants, or behind a workbench sawing planks of wood. These students weren't smiling, they were concentrating. It didn't look bad, but it was a technical school. They'd never let me in. My stomach cramps returned without warning.

•

Mr. Martineau made me a proposition: He would pay me to help him remove his old wallpaper. I accepted. We went to the tool rental shop and rented two steam wallpaper removers. Charles and Mrs. Martineau had gone on vacation, and my parents were working, so we were left in peace.

We did a good job; but it was hard work! We were having a heat wave, and I don't need to tell you what it was like being in a steam bath when it's ninety degrees in the shade. It was like being in a sauna! I drank beer for the first time and found it disgusting.

Grandpa Leon came by to give us a hand. Mr. Martineau was delighted. He said, "We are just laborers, but you are a true artist, Mr. Dubosc." So my grandfather pottered around delighting in all the subtleties of plumbing and electricity while we sweated it out, swearing like troopers.

Mr. Martineau often said, "Damnus, damna, damnum, damnorum, damnis, damnis." (It's Latin.)

•

Finally, my parents enrolled me at the

junior high school just near our house. At first, they didn't want to send me there, because it had a bad reputation. The teachers were terrible, and the students got mugged for their sneakers, but since it was the only school that would accept me, they didn't have much choice. They handed in my school records, and I went to get ID photos. I really look awful in those little photos. I told myself that the junior high school would be delighted with their new recruit: a guy of thirteen in sixth grade, with Incredible Hulk hands and a Frankenstein face. I was really some catch!

•

July flew past. I learned to paper walls: how to apply the paste and fold the sections of paper properly; how to smooth down the edges with the roller and get rid of air bubbles. I learned a lot of things. Today I can claim to be an ace at wallpapering with striped paper. I helped my grandfather to untangle the electrical wiring and try it out:

"Does it work?"

"No."

"And now?"

"No."

"Damn. And now?"

"Yes."

I made foot-long sandwiches. I varnished doors, changed fuses, and listened to comedy shows on the radio for a whole month. A whole month of happiness.

It should have gone on forever, and in September I could have started another job with another boss. . . . I was thinking of that as I tore into my salami sandwich: only three years to go, and here I come.

Three years is a long time.

•

Then there was another thing that worried me. Grandpa Leon's health. He coughed more and more often and for longer and longer. He would sit down after the slightest exertion. My grandmother had made me promise to keep him from smoking, but I couldn't do it. He would say, "Leave me my one pleasure, Toto. I'll be dead soon enough."

This kind of answer made me mad.

"That's rubbish, Toto. You'll kill yourself with your stupid 'pleasure.'"

He laughed. "Since when do you get to call me Toto, Toto?"

When he smiled at me like that, I remembered that he was the person I loved most in the world, and that he had no right to die. Ever.

The last day of the wallpapering job, Mr. Martineau invited me and grandfather to a gourmet restaurant. They smoked a giant cigar each after the coffee. I didn't dare think how my poor grandmother would have tortured herself with worry if she had seen them.

As we were about to go our separate ways, my neighbor handed me an envelope.

"Here, take this. You deserve it, you know."

I didn't open it right away. I waited till I was back home and opened it on my bed. I was absolutely stunned. I had never even seen so much money in my life, let alone had it in my possession. I didn't want to tell my parents, because they would have gone on forever about how I should put it safely into my savings account. I wanted to hide the bills where no one in the world would think to look for them, and I began to rack my brains. I thought and thought and thought.

What on earth was I going to buy with all that? Motors for my models? (They cost a fortune!) Comic books? A CD-ROM called "One Hundred Things to Build"? A Timberland jacket? A Bosch chain saw?

Those four bills made my head spin, and when we closed up the house for August to go on vacation, I spent over an hour looking for a safe enough hiding place. I was like my mother, who was running around with her great aunt's silver candlesticks. I think we were both being pretty ridiculous. After all, thieves are always sharper than we are!

5

There's nothing much to say about that August. Only that it was long and boring. Just like every year, my parents had rented a place in Brittany, and, just like every year, I had to fill up pages of exercises in my workbook. "Passport to Sixth Grade," take two.

I spent hours chewing the end of my pen, watching the seagulls. I dreamed that I turned into a seagull and flew as far as the red-and-white lighthouse on the horizon. I dreamed that I made friends with a swallow and in September, on September 4 to be exact—which just happened to be the day school started up again—we left together for the sunny south. I dreamed that I crossed oceans. That we were going—

Then I shook myself back into reality. I reread my math problem, some stupid story about sackfuls of plaster, and there I was, off in my dream again. A seagull made a direct hit on the problem . . . wham! a big white splotch ruined the whole page.

I dreamed of all I could do with seven sackfuls of plaster.

In other words, I dreamed away my day.

My parents didn't look too closely at this homework. After all, they were on vacation, too, and they didn't want to drive themselves crazy trying to decipher my spidery scrawl. All they asked me to do was stay inside every morning and spend the time sitting behind a desk.

It was all so meaningless. I covered the pages of that stupid book with drawings, sketches, and crazy plans. I wasn't bored, it was just that my life didn't interest me. I asked myself, What difference does it make where I am? I also asked, To be or not to be, what does it matter? (As you can see, I may not be a mathematician, but as a philosopher, I'm not bad!)

In the afternoon I would go to the beach with either my mother or my father, never both together. That was also part of their vacation arrangement: they didn't have to put up with each other all day long. Things were not too great between my parents. Their words often had double meanings. They made loaded remarks and gave spiteful replies, all of which landed us in a heavy silence. Our family was always in a bad mood. I dreamed of having a family like in the commercials, where everyone laughs and jokes at the breakfast table . . . but I knew no families were really like that.

When the time came for us to pack our bags and clear out the house, a feeling of relief filled the air. It was crazy. Spending a fortune to go so far away, just to be relieved to go home. I thought it was just nuts.

6

My mother got her candlesticks back, and I got my money. (Now I can tell you, I had rolled the bills up and stuffed them into the barrel of my old Action Man gun.)

The leaves turned yellow, and my stomach-ache returned.

So it was time for me to start at the new junior high.

I wasn't the oldest in my class, and I was

far from being the worst student. I gave myself a break. I stayed at the back and avoided everyone. I gave up the idea of buying a Timberland jacket, because I was sure in that place, I wouldn't keep it for long.

School no longer made me so sick. The reason was simple: I no longer felt like I was at a school. I felt more like I was in a sort of zoo day care center, where two thousand adolescents were left on their own from morning to night. I was a permanent vegetable. I was shocked at how some of the students spoke to the teachers. I made myself as inconspicuous as possible, just counting the days.

In mid-October, my mother suddenly went berserk. She couldn't stand the fact that I still hadn't laid eyes on my French teacher. She also couldn't stand my vocabulary, and said that every day I got worse and worse, that I was getting to be like an animal. She couldn't understand why I never brought home any grades, and one day she went hysterical when she came to pick me up and saw kids my age hanging around outside the shopping mall smoking joints.

The result was a mega crisis at home. Screams, tears, and much blowing of noses.

The upshot: boarding school.

After an evening of fighting, my parents had finally agreed on one thing: I was going to boarding school. Great.

That night I gritted my teeth so I wouldn't cry.

The next day was Wednesday. I went to my grandparents. My grandmother had made my favorite fried potatoes, and Grandpa Leon didn't dare speak to me. The atmosphere was miserable.

After coffee, we went into his hut. Grandpa put an unlit cigarette between his lips.

"I'm giving up smoking," he admitted.

"Not for me, of course. I'm doing it for that damned wife of mine."

I smiled.

He asked me to help him screw a pair of hinges onto a door. While I was preoccupied with the job, he started talking to me gently.

"Gregory?"

"Yes."

"So, they tell me you're going to boarding school?"

" . . ."

"You don't want to?"

" . . ."

I preferred to say nothing. I didn't want to cry like a kid in third grade.

Grandpa took the wooden panel from my hands and set it aside. He put his hand under my chin and turned my head toward him.

"Listen, Toto, listen to me. I know more than you think I do. I know how much you hate school, and I also know what goes on at home. Well, not exactly, but I can guess. I mean with your parents . . . I don't suppose that every day is a barrel of laughs."

I made a face.

"Gregory, you must trust me. I'm the one who thought of boarding school and who planted the idea in your mother's head. Don't look at me like that. I think it would do you good to get away for a bit, to see other things. You are suffocating at home with your parents. You are their only child; they have only you, and they see life only through you. They don't see how much damage they are doing by investing absolutely everything in you. I promise you, they have no idea. Actually, I think the real problem is elsewhere. If you ask me, they should start by solving their own relationship before worrying so much about you. I . . . oh no, Gregory, don't cry, I didn't want to upset you, I just wanted you to . . . oh to hell with it! I can't even take you on my lap! You're too big now. Wait, get those arms of yours out the way. *I'm* going to sit on *your* lap. No, stop crying. It would be too bad. . . ."

"I'm not upset, Grandpa Leon, it's just water overflowing."

"Oh my big baby . . . come on, it's all over. Let's pull ourselves together. We have to finish this sideboard for Joseph if we want to eat for free at his restaurant. Here, pick up your screwdriver."

I blew my nose in my sleeve.

Then, in the silence that followed, just as I was about to start work on the second door, he added: "One last thing, and I won't mention it again. What I want to say is really important. I want to tell you that if your parents argue, it isn't because of you. It's their problem, and they are the only ones to blame. You have nothing to do with it, nothing at all, got it? And I guarantee that even if you were top of the class, if you only got

As and Bs, they would still fight. They would just have to find another excuse, that's all."

I didn't reply. I slapped the first coat of Bondex onto Joseph's sideboard.

7

When I got home, my parents were going through school brochures and tapping away on the calculator. If life were like a comic strip, there would have been a bubble of black smoke above their heads. I said, "Good night," and headed to my room, but they stopped me in my tracks.

"Gregory, come over here, will you?"

From the sound of his voice, I figured

that my father was in no mood for jokes.

"Sit down."

I wondered what they were cooking up for me this time.

"You know that your mother and I have decided to send you to boarding school."

I lowered my eyes. I thought, For once there is something you agree on! About time. Too bad it has to be such a pathetic subject.

"I imagine that you're not so happy about the idea, but that's the way it is. We are at a dead end. You do nothing at school, you've been expelled, nobody wants to take you, and the local school is a disaster. We don't have much choice. But what you probably don't realize is that it's very expensive. We want you to know that we are making a sacrifice for you, a big sacrifice."

I laughed ironically inside my head: Oh . . . but you shouldn't have! Thank you, thank you, you are really too kind. Allow me to kiss your feet.

My father continued: "Don't you want to know where you'll be going?"

" . . ."

"You don't care?"

"No."

"Well, actually, we have no idea. It's really a problem. Your mother has spent the whole afternoon on the phone with no result. We have to find a school that is prepared to take you halfway through the year, and—"

"There's where I want to go," I said, interrupting him.

"Where, 'there'?"

"There."

I held out the leaflet with the picture of the students at the workbench. My mother put on her glasses.

"Where is it? Thirty miles north of Valence. . . . Great Fields Technical High

School . . . but they don't have a junior high."

"Yes they do."

"How do you know?" asked my father.

"I called."

"You?"

"Yes, me!"

"When?"

"Just before the holidays."

"You did? You actually called them? But why?"

"I just did. . . . To find out."

"So?"

"So nothing."

"Why didn't you tell us?"

"Because it's impossible."

"Why impossible?"

"Because they only accept students with good school records. My record is terrible! It's so terrible that it's not even worth the paper it's written on."

My parents said nothing. My father read

the Great Fields prospectus, and my mother sighed.

The next day I went to school as usual, and the next day, and the day after that.

I began to understand the expression "to blow a fuse."

It was exactly that. I had blown a fuse. Something in me had gone out, and everything left me cold.

I did nothing. I didn't have any ideas, I didn't even want any. I put all my Legos into a box and gave them to my little cousin Gabriel. I watched TV all the time. I gaped at miles of video clips. I lay on my bed for hours on end. I did no building. My hands hung limply by my skinny sides. Sometimes I felt like they were dead. They were just about good enough to press the buttons on the remote or pop open a can of Coke.

I was no good. I was turning into an idiot. My mom was right: soon I'd be eating hay like an animal.

I didn't even feel like going to my grand-parents'. They were nice enough, but they didn't understand. They were too old. Anyway, how could Grandpa Leon really understand my problems? No way; after all, he had always been a genius. He had never had any problems.

As for my parents, forget it. They didn't even talk to each other anymore. A couple of total zombies. I thought about doing some-thing, anything, to shake them up once and for all, to get some kind of reaction, though what that might be I didn't know. A word, a smile, a gesture. Anything. But I didn't.

I was zoned out in front of the TV when the phone rang.

"So Toto, have you forgotten me?"

"Umm . . . I didn't feel like coming over today."

"So what? What about Joseph? You promised to help me deliver the sideboard!"

Oh Lord, I had completely forgotten.

"I'm on my way. Sorry!"

"No problem, Toto, no problem. It's not going anywhere!"

Joseph treated us to a big, fancy meal at his restaurant to thank us. I had a steak Tartar the size of Mount Vesuvius with all the trimmings: capers, onions, herbs, and chili. Mmmm, delicious. Grandpa Leon looked at me smiling.

"It's good to see you eat like that, Toto. Lucky that your old ancestor exploits you now and again so you can eat like a pig."

"What about you? Aren't you eating?"

"Oh . . . I'm not that hungry, you know. Your grandmother stuffed me full of breakfast, as usual."

I knew he was lying.

After lunch we visited the restaurant kitchen. I couldn't believe the size of the pots and pans: they were gigantic. And there were huge ladles, wooden spoons the size of catapults, dozens of razor-sharp knives arranged in rows from biggest to smallest.

Joseph shouted out, "Hey! This is Titi! He's our new recruit. He's a good guy. We'll get to work on him, give him a chef's hat, and you'll see, in a few years time, those imbeciles from the Michelin guide will all be smiling at him, you mark my words! Say hello, Titi."

"Hello."

Titi was peeling millions of pounds of potatoes. He looked pretty happy. His feet had disappeared under a mountain of peelings. When I looked at him I thought, He must already be sixteen, lucky guy.

•

When he dropped me in front of the house, Grandpa Leon insisted, "Okay, so you'll do like we said, won't you?"

"Yeah, yeah."

"Don't worry about the mistakes, or the style, or your terrible handwriting. Don't worry about anything. Just tell them how you feel, okay?"

"Yeah, okay."

I started trying to write my application that very night. I must have cared more than I admitted, because I did eleven rough drafts. Even so, my letter was not a long one.

I'll show you:

To the Principal of
Great Fields Junior High School

Dear Sir,

I would like to go to your school, but I know that it is impossible because my school record is too bad.

In your school brochure, I noticed that you have workshops for mechanics and carpentry. You also have computer labs and greenhouses, etc.

Personally, I think that grades are not all there is to life. Motivation is just as important.

61

I would like to go to Great Fields because I'm sure I would be happy there. At least I think so.

I am not very big: I weigh 95 pounds of hope.

Goodbye,
Gregory Dubosc

P.S.: This is the first time I have ever begged someone to go to school. I think I must be sick.

P.P.S.: I am sending you the plans of a banana peeler that I constructed when I was seven.

I read it over and found it pretty pathetic, but I couldn't face starting over a thirteenth time.

I imagined the principal's face when he read it. He was bound to think, So who is this wise guy?" and then crumple the letter into a ball and aim straight for the trash can. I didn't feel like sending it, but I had promised Grandpa Leon, and I couldn't get out of it now.

I mailed it on the way home from school. Then when I was having my snack, I reread the brochure and saw that the "Dear Sir" director was in fact a "Dear Madam." What an imbecile! I thought to myself as I bit my cheek. What a stupid imbecile!

Ninety-five pounds of hope? Yeah, right. More like ninety-five pounds of hopeless!

•

Then it was fall break. I went to Orleans to my mother's sister, my aunt Fanny. I played on my uncle's computer, never went to bed before midnight, and got up as late as possible . . . which was whenever my little cousin jumped onto my bed shouting, "'Egos! Do 'egos? Gregory, will you come and do 'egos with me?"

For four days I built with Legos. I made a garage, a village, a boat. Every time I finished something, my cousin was as excited as could be: he would stare at it in admiration and then, wham! He would hurl my creation to the floor with all his might, smashing it into a thousand pieces. The first time, it really got on my nerves, but when I heard him laugh, I forgot all the time I had wasted. I loved to hear him laugh. It fixed my broken fuse.

My mother came to pick me up at the train station. Once we were in the car, she said: "I've got two things to tell you, one good and one bad. Which shall I tell you first?"

"The good."

"The principal of Great Fields called. She's considering you, but first you have to take some kind of test. . . ."

"Ugh! That's what you call good news? A test! What am I supposed to do with a test? Use the paper for confetti? So what's the bad news?"

"Your grandfather is in the hospital."

I was sure of it. I knew it. I had felt it in my bones.

"Is it serious?"

"They don't know. He fainted, and they're keeping him under observation. He's very weak."

"I want to see him."

"No. Not now. No one can see him for the moment. He has to get stronger first."

Mom was crying.

8

I had taken my grammar book to review on the train to Great Fields, but I didn't open it. I didn't even try to pretend. I was incapable of putting one thought in front of the other and making my brain work. The train passed miles of gigantic electricity poles, and at each one I murmured: "Grandpa Leon . . . Grandpa Leon . . . Grandpa Leon . . . Grandpa Leon . . . Grandpa Leon . . . Grandpa Leon . . .

Grandpa Leon," and between the poles I said silently: "Don't die. Stay here. I need you. Grandma Charlotte needs you, too. What would become of her without you? She'd be too miserable. And what about me? Don't die. You can't die, you have no right. I'm too young. I want you to see me grow up. I want you to be proud of me. My life is only at the beginning. I need you. And if one day I get married, I want you to see my wife and my children. I want my children to go into your shed. I want them to know your smell. I want . . ."

I fell asleep.

9

In Valence, a man came to meet me at the train. During the trip to the school, I found out that he was the gardener of Great Fields, "the groundsman," as he called it.

I was pleased to be in his van. It smelled of diesel oil and old leaves.

I had dinner in the refectory with the boarders. They were all heavyset big guys. They were nice to me and told me a lot of things about the school. The best places to hide for a smoke, how to get onto the cook's good side to get extra rations, the way into the girls' dorm through the fire escape, the obsessions of various teachers, and all that.

They laughed loudly, and they were dumb. But friendly dumb. Dumb like guys together. Their hands were full of cuts and grazes, with black grease under the nails. They asked me why I was there.

"Because no other school wants me."

That made them laugh.

"Not one?"

"Not one."

"Not even reform school?"

"Yes," I said, "not even reform school. They thought I was a bad influence on the others."

One of them clapped me on the back.

"Welcome to the club, buddy!"

Then I told them about the test I had to take the next morning.

"So what are you doing still up? Go to bed and get yourself into shape!"

I couldn't get to sleep. I had a weird dream. I was with Grandpa Leon in a fantastic park, and he was driving me crazy. He kept tugging at my clothes, saying, "So where is it, the place they hide to smoke? Ask them where it is."

At breakfast, I couldn't swallow a thing. My stomach was like lead. I had never had such a pain in my life. I was breathing incredibly slowly, and I was in a cold sweat. I was boiling and freezing at the same time.

They sat me down in a small classroom and left me alone for a while. I thought they had forgotten me.

Then a woman gave me a big test booklet to fill in. The lines danced before my eyes. I didn't understand anything. I put my elbows on the table with my head in my hands. I needed to breathe, to calm down, and to empty my head. Suddenly, I was staring at the graffiti carved into the table. There was one that said, "I like big boobs," and another next to it, "I prefer saggy ones." That made me smile, and I got down to work.

At first it was okay, but the more pages I turned, the fewer answers I found. I began to panic. The worst was a paragraph a few lines long. The instructions said, "Find and correct the errors in this text." It was awful. I couldn't see a single mistake. I really was the dumbest of the dumb. The thing was full of mistakes, and I couldn't see even one! I had a lump in my throat. It came higher and higher, and my nose started itching. I opened my eyes wide. I couldn't cry. I wasn't going to cry. *I wasn't going to*, you hear?

And then it came anyway. A great big tear that I hadn't seen coming plopped itself right there onto the test book . . . the bitch! I gritted my teeth as hard as I could, but I felt I was about to crack. I knew the dam was going to give.

It had been too long. Too long that I had held back from crying, stopped myself thinking about things. But there comes a time when it all has to come out, all that messy muddle that you keep hidden at the back of your brain, way back in the deepest recesses of your mind. I knew that once I started to cry, I wouldn't be able to stop. Everything would rush out at once: Big Doggy, Marie, and all those years at school where I had been bottom of the class. Always the village idiot. My parents who didn't love each other anymore, those endless miserable days at home, and Grandpa Leon in his hospital bed with tubes up his nose and his life seeping slowly away. . . .

I was on the verge of tears, I was biting my lips to the quick, when I heard a voice saying: "Come on, Toto, what are you doing? What's going on here? Would you mind not dribbling like a pig all over your pen! You'll drown if you start bawling."

So there it was. Now I was going mad . . . hearing voices! Hey you up there! This is a mistake. I'm not Joan of Arc. I'm just a little nobody up shit creek without a paddle.

"Okay, Mr. Self-Pity, let me know when you've finished making your scene. Then maybe we could get some work done, you and I."

What was going on? I looked around the room to see if there were any cameras or microphones. What on earth was going on? Had I ended up in the twilight zone or what?

"Grandpa Leon, is that you?"

"Who do you think it is, idiot? The Pope?"

"But . . . how come?"

"How come what?"

"Um . . . how come you're here talking to me like this?"

"Don't talk rubbish, Toto, I've always been here, and you know it. Okay, that's enough kidding around. Now concentrate a little. Take a pencil and follow the directions. Underline all the adverbs you can see. . . . No, not that one, you can see it's an adjective. Now, find the subjects . . . okay . . . make arrows to point them out. . . . Good. Now, think, find all of the prepositional phrases you can. There, look at the preposition, and there's its object, that's right. Check everything. You see, you can do it if you concentrate. Now go back to the other page. I saw some terrible mistakes in your arithmetic. They made my hair stand on end. Go on, the division, yes, do that one again. Again! Look, you've forgotten something. That's right, and now let's look at page four please. . . ."

I felt like I was in a waking dream, totally concentrated yet without the slightest stress. I was writing in a fog. It was the strangest sensation.

"There you are, Toto, I'm leaving you

now. It's time for the essay, and I know you are better at that than I am. Yes you are, honestly. So I'm leaving, but check your spelling, okay? Do the same as before and check everything. Pretend you are a word cop. You ask each word for its ID before letting it go: 'Hey you! What's your name?' 'Participial phrase, sir.' 'So, you're a participle with a complement and a modifier? What do you need in your sentence?' 'A comma, sir.' 'Right, off you go.' You see what I mean?"

"Yes," I replied.

"Young man, please don't talk aloud!" exclaimed the proctor. "You must keep silent. I don't want to hear a word!"

I read over what I had written. At least fifty-seven times. Then I gave in my book. Once I was in the hall, I whispered, "Grandpa Leon, are you still there?"

No reply.

I tried again in the train on the way

home. No way. There was no answer at the number I was calling.

When I saw my parents' faces on the station platform, I knew something had happened.

"Did he die?" I asked. "He died, didn't he?"

"No," said my mother. "He's in a coma."

"Since when?"

"Since this morning."

"Is he going to wake up?"

My dad made a face, and my mother collapsed against my shoulder.

10

I didn't go see him at the hospital. Nobody did. It wasn't allowed, because the slightest germ could kill him.

But I did go to my grandmother's, and I had a shock when I saw her. She looked even more frail and fragile than usual, like a little white mouse engulfed by her blue dressing gown. I was standing like an idiot in the middle of the kitchen when she said,

"Go and work a little, Gregory. Get the machines working. Touch the tools. Feel the wood. Go talk to his stuff. Tell them he'll be back soon."

She was crying silently.

I went in and sat down. I crossed my arms over the bench, and at last I let myself cry.

I cried all the tears that I had been holding back for so long. How long did I stay like that? An hour? Two? Maybe three?

When I stood up I felt better, as if I had no more tears left to cry, no more misery. I blew my nose in an old glue-stained rag lying on the ground, and that's when I saw the words I had carved into the wood the time I was expelled: HELP ME.

11

I got into Great Fields.

I didn't feel especially good or bad about it. I was just pleased to get away, to "get some fresh air" as Grandpa Leon would have said. I packed my bag and didn't look back when I closed the door to my room. I asked my mother to put the money from Mr. Martineau into my savings account. I no longer felt like spending it. I no longer wanted anything, except for what was impossible. And I understood that not everything in life could be bought.

My father took advantage of one of his long-distance rounds to drive me to my new school. We both realized that from now on we would go our separate ways.

"Call me if you hear anything, okay?"

He nodded, then gave me a clumsy hug.

"Gregory?"

"Yes?"

"No. Nothing. Try to be happy—you deserve it. You know, I've never said this, but I think you're a good guy . . . a really good guy."

And he hugged me hard before getting back into his car.

12

I wasn't the best in the class. I was even among the worst. If I think about it, actually I think I was at the bottom. But the teachers seemed to like me.

One day, Mrs. Vernoux, the lit teacher, gave us back our text analyses. I had 6 out of 20.

"I hope your banana peeling machine worked better than this," she said with a little smile.

I think they liked me because of that letter I had sent. Everyone here knew that I was a lousy student, but that I wanted to do well.

On the other hand, in drawing and technology I was the king. Especially in technology. I knew more than the teacher. When the others couldn't manage to do something, they would come to see me before they asked him. At first Jougloux didn't like it, but after awhile he started doing it, too. He was always asking my advice. It was really funny.

My worst thing was sports. I was always bad at it, but here it showed even more, because the others were all good, and what was more, they loved it. I was terrible at everything. I couldn't run or jump or dive or catch a ball, let alone throw it. Nothing. Zero. The bottom of the heap.

The others joked about it. They would say, "Hey Dubosc, when are you going to invent a muscle-building machine?"

Or, "Watch out, guys! Dubosc is about to jump. Get out the bandages!"

My mother called every week. At first I would ask her if there had been any news. One day she finally exploded.

"Listen, Gregory, stop. Stop asking me that. You know perfectly well that if there were any news I'd tell you right away. I'd rather hear about you, what you are doing, your teachers, your friends, all that stuff."

I had nothing to say to her. I forced myself a bit, and then I cut off the conversation. Anything that wasn't about my grandfather didn't matter.

13

I was okay, but I wasn't happy. I was frustrated at not being able to do anything to help Grandpa Leon. I would have moved mountains for him, cut myself into little pieces and fried myself up for dinner. I would have taken him in my arms and carried him across the whole world. I would have put up with absolutely anything to save him, but there you are, there was nothing to do but wait.

It was unbearable. He had helped me when I needed it most, but what could I do for him? Nothing. Nothing at all.

•

Until the infamous P.E. class.

The dish they served up that day was the rope climb. For me this was an absolute horror. I had been trying since the age of six, and I had never managed it. Not once. The knotted rope was my greatest shame.

When my turn came, Momo shrieked out, "Come and see Dubosc! He's actually going to try the rope!"

I looked to the top of the rope, and murmured, "Grandpa Leon, listen to me! I'm going to do it. I'm going to do it for you. For *you*, do you hear me?"

At the third knot I was ready to quit, but I gritted my teeth. I pulled on my pathetic scrawny arms. Fourth knot, fifth knot. I was about to let go. It was too hard. No, I couldn't do that, I had promised! I gulped and pushed on my feet. It was no good. I couldn't make it. That's when I saw them down below, all the guys from my class in a circle. One of them shouted, "Go Dubosc, you can do it!"

So I tried again. Drops of sweat blurred my vision. My hands were on fire.

"Du-bosc! Du-bosc! Du-bosc!" they chanted to encourage me.

Seventh knot. I had to let go. I felt like I was about to faint.

Down below they were still chanting for me, "Go! Go! Go!"

They certainly gave me strength . . . but not enough.

There were only two knots left. I spat in one palm then the other. "Grandpa Leon, here I am. Look! I'm sending you my strength. I'm sending you my willpower. Take it, take it all! You need it. The other day, you sent me your knowledge, well now, I'm sending you all that I have: my youth, my strength, my breath, my determination, my muscles. Take it, Grandpa Leon! Take it all . . . I beg you!"

The skin inside my thighs began to bleed, and my joints were completely numb. Only one more knot to go.

"Go! Gooo! Goooooooooo!"

The guys were going crazy. The teacher was shouting loudest of all. I yelled, "GRANDPA, WAKE UP!!!" and caught hold of the top of the pole. Below, celebration broke out. I was crying tears of joy mixed with tears of pain. I let myself slide, half falling to the bottom. Momo and Samuel caught me and hoisted me into the air, yelling, "He's number one! He's number one!"

Everyone was cheering.

I fainted.

From that day on, I was a changed man. I became determined, tough. I had a will of iron. I had drunk the magic potion.

Every evening after class, instead of

going to watch TV, I went walking. I crossed villages, woods and fields. I walked for ages, breathing slowly and deeply and always thinking: Take all this, Grandpa Leon, breathe in this air, breathe. Smell the earth and the mist. I'm here. I'm your lungs, your breath and your heart. Relax, take it all.

It was mouth-to-mouth by long distance.

I ate well and slept a lot, and I went to see the neighbor's horses. I put my hands under their thick warm manes and murmured, "Take it, it's good for you."

•

One evening my mother called. When the supervisor came to tell me, my heart sank to the depths.

"I've got bad news, honey. The doctors are stopping the treatment. It's doing no good."

"You mean he's going to die!" I yelled into the receiver for the whole hall to hear.

"Why don't you just switch him off. That way it would be quicker!"

And I hung up.

•

From that day on, I stopped my charade. I went back to playing foosball with the other guys. I worked badly and hardly spoke to anyone. Life disgusted me. In my mind, I felt like he was already dead. When my parents called again, I hung up on them.

•

Then yesterday a twelfth grader came to get me. I was in bed fast asleep. He shook me in all directions.

"Hey there, wake up, buddy."

My mouth was all gummed up.

"Whash happening?"

"Hey, are you Toto?"

"What are you asking me that for?"

I rubbed my eyes.

"Because there's this old guy downstairs in a wheelchair, and he's yelling that he wants to see his Toto. . . . He wouldn't by any chance mean you, would he?"

Wearing just my shorts, I rushed down the four floors, already sobbing like a baby.

He was there by the refectory door, with a guy in a white coat next to him. The white coat was holding the IV thing, and Grandpa Leon was smiling at me.

As for me, I was crying so much that I couldn't even manage to smile.

He said, "You should button up your shorts, Toto, you'll catch cold."

And at that, I smiled.